For Sally and now for Ben, too
P. P.

To Lizzie and Carl
W. A.

Text copyright © 1971, 2007 by Philippa Pearce
Illustrations copyright © 2007 by Wayne Anderson

First U.S. edition 2007

Library of Congress Cataloging-in-Publication Data is available.

Library of Congress Catalog Card Number 2006052454

ISBN 978-0-7636-3551-0

2 4 6 8 10 9 7 5 3 1

Printed in China

This book was typeset in Vendome Regular.
The illustrations were done in colored pencil, pencil, acrylic ink, watercolor, and a touch of magic.

Candlewick Press
2067 Massachusetts Avenue
Cambridge, Massachusetts 02140

visit us at www.candlewick.com

The Squirrel Wife

an original fairy tale by Philippa Pearce

illustrated by Wayne Anderson

CANDLEWICK PRESS
CAMBRIDGE, MASSACHUSETTS

ONCE UPON A TIME, LONG AGO,

at the edge of a great forest, there lived two brothers who were swineherds. The elder brother was very unkind to the younger brother, who was named Jack. He made Jack do all the work and gave him hardly enough to eat.

Every day in the autumn, Jack drove the pigs into the forest to eat the fallen acorns and the beechnuts and to rootle in the earth. As he set off, his brother always gave him the same warning: "Don't take the pigs deep into the forest, and be sure to bring them home before sunset, because of the green people."

The green people were the fairy people who lived in the heart of the forest, and the forest was their kingdom. They could be seen only by moonlight. Everyone feared them.

ONE AUTUMN EVENING, when Jack was bringing the herd of pigs out of the forest as usual, he noticed that a wind was beginning to whip up. It whirled the leaves from the trees and tossed their branches wildly. By the time the pigs were in their sties and Jack in the cottage, which he shared with his brother, a storm was blowing.

That night, when the two brothers had gone to bed, they could not sleep for the howling of the wind around their cottage. In the middle of the storm, they heard the crash of a great tree falling in the distance, from the direction of the forest.

"Did you hear that?" Jack whispered.

"What a fool you are, Jack!" said his brother. "Of course I heard the tree falling."

"But did you hear nothing else?" said Jack. "There it goes again—listen!"

They both listened, and over the howling of the storm came a strange voice far off, crying for help.

"There!" said Jack.

"I heard nothing," said his brother.

"But you must have heard it: someone calling from the forest."

"I tell you, I heard nothing. And if there was someone calling, this is not the kind of night to go out helping strangers. Be quiet and go to sleep, or it will be the worse for you."

So Jack held his tongue.

At last the gale blew itself out and the elder brother fell asleep, but not Jack. As soon as he heard his brother snoring, he crept out of bed and left the cottage. As he went, he stuck his wood-ax into his belt as protection against wild beasts or any other enemies.

He took the moonlit way that led to the forest. He reached the very edge of the forest, hesitated, and then plunged in.

Almost at once he came upon the great tree—a beech tree—whose crashing fall he had heard that night.

The tree lay with its trunk full-length upon the ground, its roots torn up into the air, and its leaves smashed down into the earth. It was all black and silvery gray in the moonlight, and then Jack noticed a strange greenness where there should have been none.

He looked closely and saw what at first he thought was a child—a green child—but this was a man, perfectly formed in every way and yet only the height of a child, and green. He was one of the green people.

The green man had been trapped by the fall of the tree, for it had fallen across his legs. He could not move. He stared at Jack, and Jack stared at him, but neither said a word. Jack took the wood-ax from his belt and began to hack him free. When he had done this, Jack expected the green man to escape at once back into the depths of the forest. But the green man lay as before, and Jack saw that one of his legs had been crushed by the fall of the tree.

What was to be done? Jack could not bear to carry the green man home to his cruel brother; nor could he leave him here, where his own people might never find him. Jack looked at the green man, and the green man looked at Jack, and neither said a word, but Jack knew what he must do. Although he was afraid to do it, he must carry the green man back to his own people in the heart of the forest. He picked him up in his arms—he was as light as a child—and began to carry him deeper and deeper into the forest.

At last, in the heart of the forest, Jack came to a clearing where, by moonlight, he saw a company of the green people on horseback.

Two of them came to him at once and took the injured man from him, all without a word being spoken on either side.

Then one who was clearly lord of them all beckoned to Jack.

Jack knelt, and the lord of the green people said, "Jack, you have done a good night's work and deserve to be paid for it. This is your reward: you shall enjoy the secrets of our forest through your wife."

Jack dared respectfully to point out that he had no wife, nor any thought of one as yet.

"I know that," said the lord of the green people, "just as I know that you are Jack the swineherd, living at the edge of our forest. Now take this gold ring." He took a ring from his finger as he spoke and held it out to Jack. It was a plain gold ring, like a wedding ring. Jack took it and thanked him for it, but the lord of the green people had not finished with Jack. "You will wear this ring upon your finger," he said, "until the spring comes.

"In spring the squirrels build their nests in the trees of our forest and bear their young. At that time you must climb up to a nest where there is a newborn female squirrel and put this ring over her left forepaw like a bracelet. Then come away."

"But, sir," said Jack, "would not this be a cruel thing to do? For the young squirrel will grow and the ring will stay the same size."

The lord of the green people laughed. "Jack, I think you are sometimes a fool, as your brother says. For this is a magic ring, which will grow as the wearer grows,

and at the time when squirrels are fully grown, you shall find what you shall find.

"And now, Jack, turn and follow your path home, and do not look behind you until you are within sight of it."

Jack turned as he was told.

He looked down, and there at his feet was a path, white in the moonlight, where he could have sworn there had never been one before. He followed it without once looking back, until he came to the very edge of the forest and within sight of the cottage where he lived. Then he looked back and saw that there was no path behind him. It had vanished behind him as he went forward upon it.

Jack got home and back into bed without his brother waking, so that his brother never knew what had happened that night. Nor did he seem to notice the gold ring that Jack now wore on his finger— perhaps because it was a fairy ring and invisible to him.

TIME PASSED and
time passed, and the time
came for squirrels to build
their nests in the forest.

As he had been told, Jack
climbed tree after tree.

He searched for a squirrel to which
he might give his ring. At last he found
one—a female, newborn, tiny as a rat,
hairless, and blind as yet. He slipped
the gold ring over her left forepaw,
so that it rested just above it like a
bracelet. Then he climbed down
the tree and came away.

TIME PASSED and time passed, and autumn came, when squirrels are fully grown. Jack was driving the pigs into the forest as usual, to eat acorns and beechnuts and rootle in the earth. As he went by a woodland pool that he had often passed before, he saw someone at the edge of it, kneeling. It was a girl, who was staring at her reflection in the water as if in amazement. When she heard Jack's footfall stirring the leaves and twigs on the forest floor, she sprang up at once, more like a wild animal than a woman, and stood facing him.

Jack had never seen her before. She was small for a woman, graceful and exceedingly nimble in her movement. Her hair was brown; her eyes were brown, and what made them remarkable was their strange, wild look of watchfulness.

Jack stared and stared at the strange girl. She smiled at him as though she knew him and stretched out her left hand toward him. Then he saw that she was wearing a bracelet around her wrist—a bracelet of plain gold, just like a wedding ring but, of course, much larger.

"Jack," said the girl. "You are Jack, aren't you? I am your squirrel wife."

Then with joy Jack remembered the promise of the lord of the green people. He took the hand she held out toward him, for he knew that already he loved his squirrel wife, as she loved him. They would live together always, as man and wife. They determined not to go back to Jack's cruel brother but to settle far from him, within the forest.

The forest was the only place for a squirrel wife.

And there among the trees they would live happily.

So Jack divided the herd of pigs into two equal parts. One half of the herd he beat back toward his brother's cottage; the other half he took as his rightful share.

Then, driving the pigs before them, Jack and his squirrel wife went farther and farther into the forest.

On and on through the forest they went, until at last they came almost out on the other side—the side of the forest farthest from where Jack had lived with his brother. Here Jack built them a cottage and pigsties, and here they settled.

They lived very happily, and they prospered. Jack tended the pigs as before, but now he began also to make tables and chairs and many other things from the different woods of the forest.

His squirrel wife knew all the trees of the forest: oak, ash, beech, birch, and the rest. She could tell him exactly which wood was best for each purpose.

She would set her ear to the tree trunks and could tell which tree was sound all through and which was rotten, wholly or in the smallest degree. She could lay her hand upon a tree and tell its age exactly, even before Jack had cut it down and counted its year rings. She knew where the best blackberries were to be found, and the best mushrooms. She knew where the wild bees stored their honey and—of course—where the squirrels stored their nuts. It was just as the lord of the green people had promised: Jack could enjoy the secrets of the forest through his squirrel wife.

JACK AND HIS SQUIRREL WIFE spent all their time in the forest, except when they took a pigling or a table or a chair to sell in the village just outside. The villagers bought Jack's wares, but at the same time, they distrusted him because of his wife. They were afraid of the squirrel wife on account of that strange, watchful look in her eyes. The forest woman, they called her.

Word of Jack and his forest woman was passed from that village to the next, and so from village to village, until at last it reached Jack's elder brother, far away on the other side of the forest. He was so enraged to hear of Jack's happiness that he traveled all around the edge of the forest—a journey of many days—until he reached the village where Jack was best known.

There, he spread the story that Jack was a runaway thief.

"He sells you piglings that are by rights my piglings," he said to the villagers. "For this slippery brother of mine disappeared into the forest one day, taking with him half my herd of pigs. He is a thief, and I demand his punishment."

The villagers listened and nodded and said that Jack had seemed an honest man, but then indeed how could any honest man have such a wife as Jack had? So they were willing to believe the falsehoods told them by Jack's brother, and when Jack next came to the village, they seized him and threw him into prison.

Their prison was a room with a barred window and a locked door at the top of a tower. The key of the door was given into the charge of Jack's own brother. He had a room at the bottom of the tower to sleep in. Here he hung the key of Jack's prison from a nail on the wall.

Poor Jack looked out from his prison window toward the forest; he could see it but feared he might never go there freely again. He looked downward from his window and could see his squirrel wife, for she stood at the door of the tower, weeping. The end of the day had come, and the squirrel wife now turned away from the tower toward the forest, still weeping. Jack called to her to come back, but she would not. "I must go into the forest," she said, "to find the green people."

"Oh, take care!" cried Jack. "What do you mean to ask them?"

"Nothing. I mean only to give back to them my gold bracelet."

"But then you would be a squirrel again!"

"That is what I want; that is what I need to be, if I am to help you."

"Don't go!" cried Jack, shaking the bars of his window in frenzy. "Don't go! Don't go!"

But the squirrel wife had already gone, leaving Jack in despair.

The sun set. Darkness came, and then moonlight—full moonlight—and Jack was still looking out from his prison window. Everything was quiet except for the sound of Jack's brother snoring in his bed in the room below. Then Jack heard a scrabbling sound in the ivy that grew on the prison tower. He looked down and saw, by moonshine, a squirrel, slipping through his brother's open window. The sound of snoring never stopped, but in a moment the squirrel was out again with something glinting between its teeth—a key. Now it was climbing up the ivy—up, up to Jack's window. It slipped in between the bars of the window and dropped the key into the palm of his outstretched hand. Then it leaped upon his shoulder and laid its head against his cheek.

Using the key, Jack unlocked his prison door and—with the squirrel still on his shoulder—crept out and down the stairway. He could hear his brother's steady snoring as he stole past the door where he slept. He reached the heavy outside door that would let him go free from the tower altogether. He tried it, afraid that he would find it locked, but it was not. He began to ease it open. Its hinges were rusty and stiff, and as the door opened bit by bit, they creaked. At the loudest creak, the snoring stopped.

"What is it?" called the sleepy voice of Jack's brother. "Who goes there?" Then, fully awake, he shouted, "The prisoner is escaping! Stop, thief! Stop!"

By now Jack was already clear of the tower and running as fast as he could toward the forest, with the squirrel clinging to his shoulder. After him came his brother, and after his brother came the villagers, roused from their beds and taking up the cry: "Stop, thief!"

Jack reached the trees and at once plunged among them, and his brother and all the villagers, forgetting their fear of the forest by moonlight, plunged after him. But as Jack and his squirrel fled before them deeper and deeper into the forest, the shouting behind them grew fainter. Soon they could hear it no longer.

They went on until, at last, they came to a moonlit clearing where a company of the green people was assembled. With his squirrel on his shoulder, Jack went forward.

He knelt humbly before the lord of the green people. The lord was frowning. "You have noisy friends, Jack, who follow you into our forest."

"No friends of mine, sir," said Jack, "but I ask your pardon all the same."

"Is that all you have come to ask us?"

"No, sir," said Jack, not daring yet to say more.

The lord of the green people said, "First you came to us and were rewarded handsomely with the gift of a golden ring that grew in size to a bracelet. Then— this very night—your squirrel wife came to return that gift to the givers. And now you come back together— Jack and his squirrel who was once a squirrel wife—to ask something more of us.

"Before you ask, Jack, remember this: fairy gifts cannot be given twice."

"I do not ask for the ring or for the bracelet again," Jack said, "but I want my squirrel wife."

The lord of the green people shook his head. "No, Jack. We cannot give you your squirrel wife a second time. But this we will do for you: you can have either the squirrel on your shoulder or your wife by your side. Which? You decide."

Jack was bewildered by these words and hesitated. Then he said, "Sir, a man wants a wife by his side. I choose my wife."

For the first time, the lord of the green people smiled. "I think you are not always the fool your brother calls you, Jack. You have chosen wisely. You shall have your wife, and you need fear no harm either from your brother or from the people of the village.

"We shall keep your brother safe with us in the forest until he learns a little wisdom, and we shall send the rest home to their beds. We shall wipe from their minds all memory of the evil they once believed of you both. And now, Jack, turn and follow your path home. You shall find what you shall find."

As once before, Jack turned and followed a fairy path, white in the moonlight. The squirrel was still on his shoulder, and as he went, he grew amazed at its heaviness.

At last he had to stop to rest. Then he looked over his shoulder, and—lo and behold!—he was carrying not a squirrel at all, but a young woman—his wife.

She slipped down to the ground beside him, and they hugged each other. This young woman seemed to be his squirrel wife, exactly as he had always known her, but now she pressed close to him, shivering as if in dread.

She said, "Dear Jack, I fear the forest—I don't know how I could ever have wished to live here. I have one thing to beg of you. When we get home, let us gather the herd of pigs and all your tools and our household goods, and let us take them out of the forest and settle in the village. We must live like other people, because now I am like other women."

Looking into her eyes, Jack could no longer see that strange watchfulness that had made her seem like a wild creature. It had vanished altogether. Then he knew that she was no longer partly squirrel and partly woman—a squirrel wife—she was all woman now, according to the choice he had made before the lord of the green people.

"Dear wife," said Jack, "we shall do just as you wish."

So they moved all their
belongings and settled in the village
just outside the forest. The villagers welcomed
them, for they had lost all memory of Jack and his
wife as they had once been. Jack herded pigs and made
tables and chairs as before; his wife cooked and cleaned and
minded the babies that were born, but she had lost her
knowledge of the secrets of the forest.

Nor did she wish to go into the forest again, for she said that
the tall trees made her afraid, even by daylight.

By moonlight, nobody would go into the forest, because of
the green people.

So Jack and his wife lived happily at the edge of
the forest and had children and grandchildren
and great-grandchildren.

AS FOR JACK'S ELDER BROTHER,

the green people kept him as their servant for a thousand

years, until he learned a little wisdom.